BillyTibbles
Moves Out!

Valentina (that's Mum) →
Likes a peaceful house
and high-heeled
fluffy mules.
Total glamourpuss.

↗
˙ Tom (Dad) ~ says he's
permanently harassed.
Not very good with cameras.

a
big purry
thank you
to Sue
and
Sally
×

↑
Little Baby Eric,
Wise beyond his years.
Likes purple blankets.

Billy: being silly, as usual.
Likes skateboards and
teasing Twinkle.

For Shelley and Mark

This edition produced for The Book People Ltd.,
Hall Wood Avenue, Haydock, St. Helens, WA11 9UL

First published in paperback in Great Britain by HarperCollins Publishers Ltd in 2003

1 3 5 7 9 10 8 6 4 2

ISBN: 0-00-776989-X

Collins Picture Books is an imprint of the Children's Division, part of HarperCollins Publishers Ltd.

Text/illustrations copyright © Jan Fearnley 2003

The author/illustrator asserts the moral right to be identified as the author/illustrator of the work.

A CIP catalogue record for this title is available from the British Library.

The HarperCollins website address is: www.harpercollinschildrensbooks.co.uk

Printed and bound in Thailand

Twinkle - - - →
Trainee glamourpuss.
Likes glittery things
and teasing Billy.
(Secretly covets
the high-heeled
fluffy mules)

BillyTibbles Moves Out!

Jan Fearnley

Dad's foot

Billy's botty

Collins

An imprint of HarperCollinsPublishers

Billy Tibbles' bedroom was his favourite place.

Sometimes it was tidy.

Mostly it was messy.

Billy liked mess.

Billy's sister, Twinkle, had
her own room, too.
Billy wasn't
allowed in there…

…but he didn't care.
Billy liked his room best.
He had his toys
and his books…

...and his skateboard (which he wasn't supposed to ride in the house)...

...and his squeaky, creaky bed. And best of all, Billy had it all to himself.

But things changed when Mum said to Billy,
"It's time Little Eric moved in."

Little Eric was the baby.

He slept in Mum and Dad's room, in Billy's old cot.

"He's big enough to share with you now," said
Dad. "Just think, it'll be fun, two boys together."

Billy thought about it.
He thought about
sharing with Little Eric.

About sharing his toys.
Even sharing his new
skateboard!

"It doesn't sound like
fun to me!" said Billy.
"I DON'T WANT TO!"

"Now then, Billy," said Dad, wagging his finger about. "We ALL have to share in this house – and that means YOU, too!"

The green cot was moved into Billy's room.

Billy didn't like it one bit.

"It's not fair!" he cried. "I don't like sharing!"

"All big brothers have to share," said
Mum, "and that means you, too, Billy."

So, Little Eric moved in…

…and Billy Tibbles moved out!

"Huh!" he said, "I'll show them! I'm going to find somewhere better, somewhere all to myself."

Billy tried the bathroom. But the bath was hard and
uncomfortable, the tap went
drip, drip, drip, drip – and
Twinkle kept knocking
on the door, wanting
to use the loo.

Billy tried the shed. But it was
creepy and smelled of
old wellingtons.

And Billy still had to share… with the spiders!
"Ooh," said Billy, "I'm not staying here!"
He dashed back inside…

…just in time for a bedtime story.

But Twinkle wouldn't share, not even for a story.
She pushed and shoved and Billy wriggled and kicked.

"I've told you before!" Dad said. "We all share in
this house, and that means you, Billy –
and YOU, too, Twinkle!"

Dad sent them off to bed. It was dark on the stairs.
Shadows crept and lurked in every corner. For the
first time, Billy was glad he wasn't by himself.

He held Twinkle's paw tightly.

As they padded down the landing, they could hear a funny noise. It was coming from Billy's room.

Squeak... creak... *Boing!*

"Ooooh, Billy," whispered Twinkle. "I bet it's a monster. A huge monster!"

"Don't be daft," said Billy. But he squeezed Twinkle's paw even tighter, just in case.

Squeak... creak... *Boing!*

went the noise again.

"Let's see if it's a monster!" said Twinkle. "You go first, Billy."

They tiptoed to the door and peeped inside...

…and there *was* a little monster, (well, Little Eric) wide awake, and having a lovely time bouncing about on Billy's bed!

"Hey!" yelled Billy. "Get off my bed!"

"Nah!" said Little Eric. "Don't want to!"

Billy pounced… *Grrrr!* and Billy bounced…

...very, very, very high.
It was brilliant!

And when Twinkle joined in, it was even better.
Squeak... Little Eric made a star shape.
Creak.... Twinkle did a somersault.
BOINNNG! Billy nearly cracked his head on the ceiling. But he didn't mind – it was excellent!

squeak!

creak!

boing!

Meanwhile, Mum and Dad were looking
forward to a nice relaxing evening.

"Peace and quiet at last!" sighed Dad.

"I wonder how the kids are getting on?"
said Mum. "What's that funny noise?"

"Can't hear a thing," yawned Dad.

Creak.

Boing!

Squeak.

Boing!

CRRACK!

"Right!" said Dad. "That's it!"

"What is going on?" roared Dad. "Why aren't you asleep?"

"The bed's broken," said Twinkle.

"How did that happen?" asked Mum.

"We were sharing," said Billy. "Dad told us to."

"I'm bouncing!" said Little Eric.

Mum raised a weary paw.

"No more explanations," she sighed.

"They'll give me a headache.

It's very late.

We'll sort things out in the morning. The boys can
share with us tonight."

"Me too!" said Twinkle. "I like sharing."

Dad didn't look too happy about it. "Sharing?
With this lot?" he groaned. "I don't want to!"

"Now then, Dad," said Billy, wagging a cheeky
finger, "remember, everybody shares in our house –
AND THAT MEANS YOU, TOO!"

So Dad moved over to make room, because Dads have to share, just like everyone else.

The children leapt aboard the big, cosy bed and, eventually, everybody had a very good night's sleep.

Well, almost everybody.